GAME PLAN

TONYA CLARK

CHAPTER ONE
LUCAS

ANOTHER WIN IN THE BOOKS. Colorado Storm is undefeated in the MLS. The locker room is energetic and loud. Winning today's Western Conference Final puts us in the MLS Cup and a couple of these guys in the sights for the USA men's team.

The owner of the team hired me on as head coach three years ago and there hasn't been a day since that my life hasn't revolved around coaching this soccer team, trying to prove they made the right decision hiring me on. Of course with coaching you can never depend on having a job the next day, it all depends on how the team is performing, and I'm determined to make them the best.

Standing at the doors of the locker room, I look in as the guys are celebrating around the room. Kasen, the first player I signed to the team, is sitting there, his head swiveling side to side as he watches the celebration happening around him. He is the MLS's first deaf goal-keeper and that guy is a huge part of why we are where we are. I heard about him when he was in college and watched him play his last year. I knew the moment I had a team I would do just about anything to bring that guy on. It took a little convincing but after a couple play clips everyone was on board. He is probably one of the best keepers I've ever seen and he proves it game after game.

"Coach," Ryker, who is sitting next to Kasen, yells at me, "this means that there is a party at my house when we get back. Who's on the game plan for tomorrow night?"

My head falls and I shake my head as my defense player puts me on the spot. My dating life is now officially labeled the "game plan" thanks to Ryker. He swears that I have a plan, similar to the one I use from games, but instead of field positions, it's labeled with days of the week and I have a girl for each one. I'm branded a player, but I look at it as you can't get let down if you don't have any plans for the future to be broken.

Coaching is a twenty-four hour, seven days a week kind of job. If I'm not on a field, I'm home planning, watching, or reviewing. I found out just over three years ago that trying to be in a serious relationship doesn't work when you are married to your team.

I had a fiancée, the wedding was being planned, but then I got the call to coach professionally. With that offer it meant moving to Colorado, home state of Storm. That night's conversation led to a ring being handed back and me realizing that as busy as I was coaching, at the time college soccer, I wasn't aware that my soon-to-be wife was playing the field as well. Moving to Colorado meant moving away from her side boyfriend. She picked him over me. Right now coaching is my first priority.

"Coach, you can't miss out on this party. We have the right to celebrate and you need to be there," Jared, our midfielder, breaks through my thoughts.

"I'm pretty sure the hotel bar is going to be busy with your celebrating tonight," I point out the obvious. "I thought parties only happened after home games?"

"This is a special exception." Ryker pats Kasen on the back, once he looks up Ryker's hands begin to move.

Kasen just shakes his head and rolls his eyes at his friend.

Coaching was in the plans, but not this early in life. I planned on playing longer than I did. I played soccer since I could walk, a ball always at my feet my mom said. Club as a kid, high school and college, and one very short season in MLS. All it takes is one injury. That's how fast you can go from player to coach.

I could have sulked and hid after my dreams of playing professional were shattered the same way my knee did, but my biggest fan, my grandmother, always said, "Everything happens for reason."

It's nothing real inspirational, or uncommon to say, but it came from the woman I respected more than anything and choose to believe I was supposed to do more than just play.

Coaching has been an experience and right now watching the players I've coached celebrate the grueling training I've put them through has me realizing this is what I'm meant to do.

"Come on, guys, get your showers," I change the subject. Turning to the door, I push through before anyone else can make another comment about my dating life.

CHAPTER
TWO
EMMA

ALL I WANT to do is get home. My flight has been canceled twice and right now I'm sitting in this hotel room praying that I finally get out on the one tomorrow morning.

I hate to fly to begin with and now this. Looking around the room, this isn't where I want to be right now, it's too depressing. I saw a little place to eat and I think a bar, maybe I should go down, get something to eat and maybe a drink to calm my nerves.

I only got on a plane to come and visit my sister and new niece, thanks to Mother Nature I'm having a heck of a time getting home. Looking out the hotel window and watching the rain pelt against the glass, I'm thinking I need that drink.

Grabbing my ID and credit card out of my wallet, I shove them into my back pocket. Grabbing my phone and card key off the nightstand, drink, here I come!

. . .

The little restaurant/bar is crowded. There is a group of guys taking up most of the space. Cheering, yelling and laughter is pouring out into the lobby. Not sure what's going on but they are celebrating something.

Walking in, I spot one lonely, empty stool at the bar. Quickly making my way through the crowd, I claim it before anyone else can.

"Hello and welcome," the bartender yells over all of the noise, "what can I get you?"

"Do you have a menu I can look at?" I yell back.

Nodding, he reaches under the bar and sets one in front of me. "I'll be back in a few."

Giving him a quick nod of understanding, I flip over the menu and search out what looks good.

"Well hello there," a male voice comes from behind me.

Looking over my shoulder, I find a group of guys all smiling at me, but they are pushing one to make the move.

"Guys, settle down. Leave the lady alone," the man who is occupying the stool next to me cuts in before I can say anything.

"Ah, come on, Coach, we are trying to teach young Adam here how not to be so shy."

Turning in my stool, I now get a better look at the group. The one they are referring to does look younger than the rest of them, with his baby face, blond hair and blue eyes. I can't help but smile at the young kid, he looks terrified.

"I'm flattered, but just looking at getting something to eat, that's all." I clarify that I'm not interested as nicely as possible. He looks like a sweet kid.

I can't help but laugh a little when I see the relief in his eyes. The group turns and walks away, leading him by the shoulders. I have a feeling his relief is going to be short lived once they spot a new target.

"I'm sorry about that. They are celebrating, some have had a few too many already," the guy sitting next to me explains.

I wave it off. "It's no big deal. What are they celebrating?"

"Today's win. They are the Colorado Storm soccer team. Just won today's game."

I'm not really into sports, but I've heard of our home state soccer league, they have been on the news quite a bit lately.

"Well, congratulations. I heard them say coach, so I'm going to assume that's who you are?"

His smile stretches across his face and those blue eyes light up with pride, "Yes, they call me Coach, but I like to introduce myself as Lucas."

I take his outstretched hand, "I'm Emma."

He looks around. "Here alone?"

"Yes, just traveling through, hoping to catch my flight in the morning."

This man is striking. Is that a word I should use to describe a man? Not sure but it's the one that first comes to mind.

His dark brown wavy hair hangs slightly over his forehead and his blue eyes can easily put a person in a trance. It's hard to look away from them, but I manage as I bring my attention back to the menu in front of me, acting as though I'm looking it over.

"Are you ready to order?" The bartender is back.

"Um, yes. Can I please have the cheeseburger, fries and a beer, anything on tap is fine. Thank you."

"Put it on our ticket," the man next to me instructs the bartender.

"Thank you, but that's not necessary."

"Please, as an apology for my players."

"They didn't do anything wrong."

He gives the bartender a slight nod to confirm. The man just smiles and walks away.

CHAPTER
THREE
LUCAS

THIS RED-HAIRED, green-eyed, melt you to your knees woman sitting next to me has something about her that is pulling me in. Once I turned around and noticed who the guys were trying to pick up on, I realized what caught their attention to begin with. She is breathtaking.

What…breathtaking? Where did that come from? That's not my usual way to describe any woman.

As the hours pass, the guys are dropping a couple at a time. Between the game, the energy it takes to celebrate and the beer, I'm probably going to have to stop at a few rooms in the morning just to make sure the guys are making it to the bus on time to get us to the airport.

My attention has mostly been on Emma. We've talked about everything and nothing really. Actually, now that I think about it, I think I've been doing the talking and it's probably all been about the soccer team, but she is listening.

Looking down at my watch, damn, it's almost one in the morning. Looking around, I have two players sitting at a table, but with their heads down and I'm going to assume passed out.

Turning my attention back to Emma, I hook my thumb over my shoulder, "I should probably get those two up to their rooms."

I would much rather stay down here and talk to Emma, but I'm pretty sure I'm going to be asked to take care of them soon anyway.

"How are you going to get them both to the room? They look passed out."

Turning in the stool, I stand and make my way over to the table. Emma has followed me. "The good news is, they are bunking in the same room, so that makes it a little easier."

Isaac's head pops up from the table at the sound of our voices, "Coach."

Well, that makes things a little easier, at least one is somewhat conscious. "Hey, bud, it's time we get you two up to your room."

Isaac slaps Jared on the arm and yells, "We have to go!"

Jared moans a little but nothing else.

"All right, boys," I grab Jared by the arm and pull him up from his chair.

He manages to get to his feet and put his arm around my shoulder. I laugh at the thought of how much he is going to hate life in the morning and the plane ride home. Serves him right, probably should make sure he is close to the bathroom.

Damn, I have to pay the tab. Jared is draped against me and I can't seem to be able to reach around for my wallet out of my back pocket.

Looking at Emma, I smile, "I know we just met, but mind grabbing my wallet out of my back pocket?"

She gives me a wicked grin that has my knees about buckling, "Now that's a line I haven't heard before."

She walks around and I feel her fingers lightly brush the backside of my jeans as though she is trying very hard not to touch me. The wicked grin was just a teaser, she might be a little more shy than she lets on.

Coming back around to the front of me, she hold my wallet up to me.

"Thank you," I say as I take it from her and flip it open, pulling out my card and handing it to her. "Mind taking that to the bartender?"

CHAPTER
FOUR
EMMA

HE GIVES me an apologetic smile as I take the card from him and make my way over to the bar.

The bartender gives me a tired smile as he takes it and steps away with the card to close out the tab. I can only imagine how tired that man is. Only one working and he kept up with this group. I'm pretty sure once we are gone he gets to go home.

It only takes a moment, the bartender is back. "Thank you, have a nice rest of your evening."

"You, too."

Returning to the table, Lucas has both guys on their feet, the one still draped over him and the other swaying back and forth but standing on his own two feet.

Handing him his card, he places it back into his wallet and hands it to me, "Would you mind?"

"Sure." I take the wallet, skipping the whole trying to give a sexy grin thing again. I'm pretty sure I wasn't that sexy the first time.

Walking around him and his player, I place his wallet back into his back pocket, taking an extra moment to appreciate the sight before me. My hands itch to tuck into those pockets and squeeze just a little.

"Thank you, I appreciate all of your help. As much as I'd rather keep talking with you, I better get these two up to the room before that one can't stand on his own anymore either." He nods his head to the one he called Isaac.

I watch him sway on his feet, his eyes only half open. "Why don't I follow just in case?"

I surprise myself a little with the offer. I don't really know this man, but the way he cares for his players tells me a lot about what kind of person he is.

"The extra help would be nice."

Lucas turns and starts heading out of the bar, the player attached to him following but dragging his feet. The other just stands here, I'm not too sure that his eyes aren't closed.

Holding out my hand, I tell him, "I think you are supposed to follow them."

A small smile spreads across his lips and he takes my hand like a child would. I tug slightly and we follow after Lucas, meeting up with him at the elevator.

"I'm sorry, they are good guys," he defends both of the guys.

"It sounds like it was something to celebrate." I smile up at him.

The elevator dings and the doors open up on the third floor. Perfect, this is my floor as well.

Following, we make it to the room, I help with getting the door open and wait outside as Lucas gets the guys inside. Isaac followed them in without me.

It doesn't take long before the room door is opening again and Lucas is coming back out.

"Thank you again for the help."

Waving him off, I assure him, "It's no big deal, glad I could help."

"Can I at least walk you back to your room?"

A gentleman, that's something you don't see a lot these days, it's refreshing. "Thank you."

We make our way down the hall but I stop only four rooms away. Taking my card key out of my back pocket, I look up and smile, "Thank you."

Lucas laughs, "Well, at least you know it will be quiet, the whole team is on this floor I think, but I'm sure they are all passed out."

I put my hand out, "Well, Lucas, soccer coach of the famous Storm team, it was very nice meeting you."

His hand takes mine and what feels like a bolt of electricity shoots up my arm. What the heck was that? It surprises me so much that I don't even attempt to stop him as he pulls me in and before I know it his lips are claiming mine.

That same electricity that shot up my arm just bolted from his lips, through mine and about buckle my knees from under me. My other hand comes up and fists into his shirt and I hear the mixture of both our moans fill the hallway as his tongue finds mine.

The key I'm holding against his shirt is removed from my hand and I'm slightly aware that we are moving now.

I hear the heavy hotel room door shut and I'm now pressed back against it, Lucas's body tight against mine.

His lips are intoxicating with the taste of the beer he was drinking, now mixed that with the scent of whatever musk he is wearing and the solid mass of muscles that are pressed tight to me, I'm finding it very difficult to remember this isn't like me at all. I'm not a one-night stand kind of person, but I can't seem to find it in me to push him away.

Push him away…it's me that works my hands under his shirt, finding the warm skin of his abdomen, his muscles flexing under my fingers as they explore each ripple in turn. Pushing his shirt up, or lips separate only long enough for me to pull his shirt up over his head, letting it fall from my hands so that my fingers can go back to exploring the path of muscles they began to follow.

My shirt and bra are quick to follow his and the moment our skin touches, the fire building throughout my body all collects in my core.

Lucas easily lifts me up, my legs wrapping around his waist. I can feel his hardness through both of our jeans. His mouth sucks one tight nipple and my head falls back against the door, my fingers digging into his hair silently pleading for more.

If I had one second to think I would be stopping this, but there isn't time to think, only feel and it's like nothing I've felt before. I'm no saint, I've been with men, but nothing like this.

I'm not even aware that he has pulled me away from the door until he dips me down, my back pillowed by the bed.

Lucas makes short work of both our remaining clothes and before I know it, my legs are wrapped tight around him and he is bringing me to a release I didn't know was possible.

CHAPTER
FIVE
LUCAS

THERE IS A MUFFLED beeping sound pounding in my head. I didn't have that much to drink last night, so why do I feel like I've been run over by a Mac truck? Opening my eyes just enough to look around the room, it's still pitch black, it can't be morning already.

Wait…hotel room, game, flight this morning, her lips, body, sounds. I'm not in my hotel room, but as I stretch my arm out to my left, I find I am in a bed, alone.

Hitting the light switch on the light next to the bed, it lights up the room and there's the proof, I'm alone. This is Emma's room, so where did she go?

The beeping sound that woke me up is my phone's alarm clock going off, it's still in the pocket of my jeans somewhere on the floor.

Looking over the room there isn't one thing that proves Emma was here. There is no luggage, no clothing, nothing. Looking at the door, I do remember this morning's activities and I'm not in my room, so it all happened.

Grabbing my jeans off the floor, I pull my phone out, swiping the screen to stop the annoying beeping that is only getting louder the longer I ignore it.

Shaking my head, I can't believe she just left. Something tugs at my gut, what the hell is my problem? This should be ideal. Great night, amazing woman, no odd morning goodbyes, this is what my life is about right now, but I'm feeling a lot of different things and none of them are relief.

Running my hands over my face a couple times, I realize I don't have the time to sit here and dwell on it either. Pulling on my pants, grabbing my shoes, and picking up my shirt that is still on the floor, I make my way out of this room and down to mine which just happens to be a couple of doors down the hall.

They may not all be awake, or smiling, but all the guys make it down to the bus and we make it to the airport in plenty of time to check in and get through the security check.

I've had little time to think about Emma and when I did find myself thinking about her, I felt like slapping myself. I'm not one to get twisted up over a woman. I probably would have been the one walking out without saying goodbye this morning if I would have woken up first, but something is knotting up in my chest and I have caught myself reliving that bedroom scene over and over again in my head. This is insane.

Leaning forward, I brace my arms on my knees and drop my head into my hands, but this isn't helping. I close my eyes and I can see her head back against the door, feel her

GAME PLAN 19

legs wrapped around my waist, and taste the sweetness of her skin as I played with one tight nipple with my tongue. No woman should taste that amazing.

"Coach, you good?" Calvin plops down in the seat next to me.

Nodding my head in my hands, I take a deep breath and look up, "I'm good, just ready to be home."

"I feel you on that. I'm not sure how late some of these guys stayed out, but I didn't stay long, yet I still feel like I'm dragging."

The speakers above us crackle a little and then a female voice announces, "Flight 324 to Denver, Colorado is now boarding at gate 4."

"That's us, let's make sure all of these guys are awake and make it on the plane." I recruit Calvin to help out. I don't want to be up in the air when I realize one of these guys is still sleeping in a chair here in the airport.

All players accounted for and in their seats, I'm running through emails as the rest of the passengers load the plane. The seat next to me is empty and I'm not going to lie, I'm kind of hoping it stays that way.

"I'm sorry, that's my seat next to you."

That voice is quiet and smooth, and a little shaky, but I'd know it blindfolded. Looking up from my phone, a lady is standing next to me, reaching up above me stowing her luggage. She is wearing a ball cap and baggy sweatshirt, but my body instantly reacts to her, like it knows her scent and her sound. The red hair confirms it.

Standing, I reach above the two of us, "Here, let me help you with that."

The body now pressed to mine goes stiff and I hear her surprised intake of breath that she takes. Pushing her suitcase into the cubby, I bring my arms down and onto each side of her waist, pulling her in just a little tighter to me.

"Good morning, Emma."

Her head stays down so that the bill of the hat is covering her face, but I feel her hands clutch around the sides of my shirt. I can't help but smile a little knowing she is as affected by me as I am her.

"Excuse me, can we get past?" An older lady and her husband are impatiently waiting for us to clear the small aisle so that they can get to their own seats.

Adjusting my body into the isle, I release my hold on Emma and hold a hand out to her seat, waiting for her to take her seat by the window.

She quietly apologizes to the older couple, embarrassment in her voice, as she quickly takes her seat. I follow and take mine, now opening up the aisle for people to get by.

I watch as she settles into her seat, puts on her seatbelt and then turns her head to look out the window as though she has no idea who I am, instead of the man that just spent a couple of hours this morning memorizing her body.

CHAPTER SIX
EMMA

THIS CAN'T BE HAPPENING. This can't be happening. I'm pretty sure no matter how many times I keep saying it the man sitting next to me isn't going to disappear.

This morning I woke up, naked, in bed next to a guy that just showed me a night that will forever ruin it for anyone else that is in my future.

Sleeping with a guy I had only known for maybe five hours isn't my norm. I lay there waiting to feel regret, but it never happened. I didn't regret one thing about the time I had with Lucas, but I knew I couldn't stand waking up together and moving on with our day like nothing happened and knowing we were never going to see each other again. So, I got up and got out as quickly and quietly as possible. My body has been humming from my multiple releases all morning, creating a constant reminder of what Lucas made me feel.

I arrived so early to the airport that I feel asleep waiting to board. Slept through the boarding call and luckily the woman across from me was watching out for me, because if she wouldn't have woken me up, I would have missed my flight and been stuck, again.

When Lucas placed his hands on each side of my waist and pulled me tight to him, I almost moaned out loud in the middle of a full plane as my body remembered every inch of him against me.

What were the chances that I would be on the same flight, let alone sitting right next to him? I knew he was from Colorado as well, but there is more than one airport. Dropping my head against the back of the seat, I close my eyes. Can this nightmare of a situation get any worse?

Big mistake, the smell of whatever he is wearing that makes me want to climb in his lap and beg for more fills my nose and last night instantly replays like a movie behind my closed eyes.

My arms are crossed over my chest, my legs are smashed against the wall of the plane and I'm acting like Lucas is a complete stranger, instead of the guy that has had his lips on every inch of my body.

He hasn't said a word to me since we sat down. Do I blame him? He probably thinks of me as a…

The flight attendant comes over the loudspeaker stopping all thoughts. Now my nerves are starting to kick into overdrive.

As she goes through the little spiel about what to do in case of an emergency, my heart begins to beat faster and faster.

I'm squeezing my eyes shut now. Man, I hate flying, but seeing my niece was worth it and if I'm completely honest with myself, last night was completely worth it.

The plane starts to roll back and my hands go to both armrests and I hold on tight. My leg is bouncing so hard I'm surprised they can't feel it throughout the whole plane.

The plane taxis out, picking up speed and then begins to lift off the ground and I feel myself holding my breath. I just have to get through the takeoff. Once it levels out, I can usually distract myself with a movie.

A sense of protection runs through me as something warm and strong takes hold of my hand. My hand squeezes tight, trying to pull that warmth to the rest of my body. A soothing touch brushes lightly over the back of my hand and my heart begins to slow down.

I'm drawn to the warmth, my head falls to the right until it lands on something solid, my body curls around the warmth at my side, but my eyes remain shut and my hand a death grip on whatever is holding it.

The plane dips slightly and I have to bite my tongue to hold back the small scream that threatens. I find myself now hiding my face between the seat and the warmth.

I hear the soft whispers, but I can't tell you what is being said. I feel the light touches on my forehead. My body begins to relax once again with the sense of protection that I don't want to move away from.

CHAPTER
SEVEN
LUCAS

THE MOMENT the plane starts to move, I see the change in Emma. Her breathing becomes rapid, her knee is bouncing and she has a death grip on the armrest of the chair. She may not want to talk to me, but I can't just sit here and watch her go through the quiet panic attack.

When I move my hand and touch hers she instantly lets go of the armrest and grabs it. I push the armrest between us up and move my body as close to hers as the seatbelt will allow. She never says a word or opens her eyes, but her body curls up to mine and her breathing starts slowing down a little.

Her fingernails are biting into my hand, but if it makes her feel safer, I'm good with the pain it's creating.

I adjust my body so that anyone from the aisles on the other side of us can't see her and I wait and hold her as the plane takes off.

The plane starts to level out and I feel her relax even more. Her nails are no longer marking my skin. Kissing her forehead, I let her know she is safe and that I've got her. She hasn't said a word, she still has her eyes closed, but her body has relaxed into mine.

Having her curled up to me has my body remembering last night, the soft curves of her body curled up alongside of me, her head on my chest, her legs tangled with mine. It wasn't the norm for me, I'm not usually a person that lays around cuddling.

I know the guys like to think of me as a player, tease me about my game plan, but it's more like I don't really use woman, I just don't get too close.

It's not like I go out looking for a different girl every night, I just don't stay around long once I'm with one. I don't cuddle, I don't hang around for morning coffee, or breakfast, lie there making small talk.

Hell, last night I wasn't even looking to kiss Emma goodnight. It's not always about sex with me either. I enjoyed the small conversations we had at the bar, I appreciated her help getting the guys to their room.

It was something about the way she looked up at me when we got to the door to her room, I wasn't ready to say goodbye.

Then there was this morning. I was actually disappointed when I woke up alone. My chest felt tight as I looked around the room and realized everything of hers was gone.

The plane levels out and I hear Emma take a large deep breath and slowly let it out. She doesn't move, though, and

I'm all right sitting here like this the whole flight if that's what she needs.

Her hand pulls away from mine but only to take it into her hand and lightly rub her thumb over the marks left by her nails.

"I'm so sorry." Her voice is quiet. She doesn't move her head from my shoulder.

"It's not a problem."

"But you're bleeding."

"It's just a reminder of this woman I met last night. She kind of ran away from me this morning."

She brings my hand up to her lips and lightly kisses over the angry marks.

"There are a couple along my upper arm that match these."

Her movement freezes and I can't help but laugh. Her head bends back against my shoulder as she looks up at me. It's the first time she has looked at me.

"I'm just looking at them as reminders of a great evening." I smile down at her.

Her cheeks turn a light shade of red and she pulls her bottom lip between her teeth as she tries to hide her smile.

"Why did you leave?"

She shrugs, "I didn't want to be that girl who slept with the random guy and has the awkward morning after. I don't usually sleep with men I've met a couple of hours before."

Taking my hand from hers, I use my knuckles under her chin to tilt her head back just enough to lightly kiss her lips. Testing if she's going to pull away or not. When she doesn't, I deepen the kiss. A very soft whimper has me smiling against her lips.

"If you wouldn't have left, there could have been a little more than just this between us this morning," I say against her lips.

"I couldn't risk missing my flight this morning." Her head lays back onto my shoulder and her eyes close.

Within moments her breathing has evened out and I'm pretty sure she has fallen asleep.

Something tugs in my chest. She started to calm the moment I took her hand and now nestled into my side, she has actually fallen asleep. It's speaking volumes, only problem is I'm starting to fight it in my own head.

Every action starting from last night from the moment I took her lips, I've been in uncharted territory for myself when it comes to women and relationships. Every rule I've made for myself has been broken and I'm realizing I'm all right with it.

The wheels touch down on the runway. Kissing Emma's forehead, I figure I better wake her up now. "Hey, we've landed."

Emma startles and sits straight up in her seat, looking around a little disorientated.

"Are you all right?" I ask.

She only nods, grabbing her bag from the floor below her and rummaging through it, but never takes anything out. She's just busying herself and ignoring me.

So we are back to this, are we?

As we taxi in, I give her the time to look for whatever imaginary thing she is looking for.

The plane's captain comes over the loudspeaker, thanks everyone for flying and the doors open. As the passengers begin to file off, our time comes and I step into the aisle and give Emma room to scoot out. Grabbing her bag and mine from above, I hand it to her.

"Thank you," she says quietly and then turns and starts to walk down the aisle, exiting the plane. I'm right behind her.

Once we make it out into the airport, Emma starts to weave her way through the crowd but I quickly catch up, taking her by the arm.

"Hey…"

She stops, takes a deep breath and looks up at me like I'm taking up her time.

It's almost enough for me to just let her go, but again something is pulling me to her.

"Can I at least have a last name?"

Her eyes search mine as she fights within herself if she is going to answer me or not.

"Thorton," she says.

"Can I see you again?"

A small smile kicks up the corner of her lips, "If you can find me. You like the game, right, Coach?"

She surprises me with this sudden playful side. She isn't being sarcastic, or rude. She isn't running pre-say. Although I do believe she may be testing me in a way. Normally that would be a huge turn off for me, I don't play games, but something is behind those eyes. This isn't the normal girl's game, she's protecting herself.

"Can I have a little hint as to where to start?" I decide to play along, something tells me she is worth it.

The smile that stretches across her face is beautiful, "I'm a teacher."

With that she pulls away from my hold and walks away, I watch as she weaves in and out of the crowd until she disappears.

CHAPTER
EIGHT
EMMA

I'M SITTING at my desk grading the test from today when the door to my classroom opens up. The bell rang to end the day about fifteen minutes ago and I'm expecting a student who may have forgotten something, but instead see Devyn, one of our newer teachers standing there.

She teaches English and coaches the girls' soccer team. Soccer coach, my chest tightens a little.

I don't know what I was expecting. I gave the man absolutely no information. He asked and I basically made a game out of it. No guy likes games and I'm sure Lucas is no exception to that. The man probably has his pick of woman, which is one of the reasons I didn't throw myself right into that mixing pot.

Adam, my fiancé, died in a small plane crash almost two years ago and even though I've been on a couple dates in the past six months, it just hasn't felt right.

Last week when I met Lucas, something shifted inside of me. Something pulled me to him and it scared the crap out of me, not going to lie, but losing Adam was almost my complete undoing and having any feelings for anyone is still something I fight with. I didn't want to give Lucas the sad story or love lost, so instead I played a game.

In the past week I've smacked myself for that a few times. I know where I can find him, I just haven't gotten up the nerve to make the first move.

"Devyn, how are you?" I distract myself from my thoughts.

"It's been one of those days," she says as she walks across the room and sits down at one of the desks across from mine.

It's at this moment that it clicks. Holy crap...Devyn's boyfriend...he found me!

"Emma, are you all right?"

I don't want to get my hopes up. "I'm good. Sorry, I was thinking of something from earlier."

"So, I said I wasn't going to get into the middle of this, but when my boyfriend and brother gang up on me, it kind of makes is impossible for me to stay out of it."

"Brother?" I ask, a little confused.

She nods, "Yes, my brother, Ryker, and my boyfriend, Kasen, both play for the Colorado Storm soccer team. My brother being as nosy as he is says that you were there at the hotel they stayed at last week and...how do I say this?" She looks around, uncertain how to continue.

"Yes, I met the coach," I help her out.

"So it was you?"

Devyn and I became fast friends. I can't say we hang out on our days off or anything, but at work we talk a lot in the teachers' lounge, she knows a little about my story and I know about hers.

Sitting back in my chair, I begin to chew on the cap to my pen, which is something I do when I'm nervous. It's a nasty habit.

"Care if I ask what happened?"

Shrugging, I can't help the small smile when I remember for the hundredth time this week that night we shared.

"Let's just say, somehow that man caught me with my guard down. Then was my savior during the flight home and then I became one of those girls no one likes and started playing games. I didn't want to be just another girl to him."

My hopes fall when I realize she said her brother and boyfriend talked to her. Lucas wasn't looking for me.

"My brother is a player, Lucas is more just protective. The guys like to tease him, but he really is a great guy. His players respect him and yes, I'm not going to lie, I've seen him with a few different ladies, but it's not like he has multiples hanging onto his arms or anything."

"But he didn't send you to talk to me?"

"He has no idea that we work together. Kasen is really good at reading lips, something to keep in mind for the future when you are around him. Anyway, I guess they saw something between the two of you and he and my brother have decided to play matchmaker."

"How did they figure out we worked together?"

"They asked if I had a way to find a teacher, long story short, they said your name and I couldn't help myself either. It's kind of fate if you ask me."

I laugh, "Fate, it was one night and a plane ride."

"Emma, Lucas is a really nice guy, I think you should give him a chance. They have practice today. If we leave now, we can get there just as it's ending. I can get us onto the fields. I have a couple connections."

Devyn herself had to learn to open her heart again. We had two different situations but opening up to something new once you have been hurt is the same no matter what. She is asking me to trust her and give this a chance. Maybe I should.

"Okay." That one word sounds so heavy.

CHAPTER
NINE
LUCAS

PRACTICE IS over and all I want to do is grab a burger on the way home and enjoy it with a beer. I'm exhausted. I haven't been sleeping. Every time I shut my damn eyes, a redheaded angel appears and reminds me of that one night.

"Coach, just remember I'm one of your favorites and you can only be mad for a minute." Ryker comes trotting up to me.

"Do I even want to know what you are talking about?"

"Well, the other night you came to the celebration party alone."

Yes, I heard about it all night. It wasn't the first time I showed up without a date, but for some reason Ryker found the evening's amusement with it.

"I figured it had something to do with that redhead from the flight home…"

"What would make you think that?"

"Kasen and I were seated behind you, those seats don't allow much privacy and in the airport after we landed, I used my best friend's superpower." Ryker shows no shame in eavesdropping into my conversation with Emma, using Kasen's ability to read lips.

Rolling my eyes, I ask, "Where are you going with all of this, Ryker?"

He points behind me. Turning, I see Devyn, Kasen's girlfriend and…holy shit, Emma.

"It just so happens they teach at the same school," Ryker says over my shoulder.

I watch as Emma spots me and stops, but Devyn says something to her and they chat back and forth a minute. Now would be a great time to have Kasen's superpower handy. Devyn gives Emma a slight push, sending her toward the field.

I meet her at the edge of the touchline and there are no words that I can say that would describe what's happening inside about seeing her again. All I know is I'm not going to fight it and I'm not going to let her walk away from me again.

I don't even give her a chance to say anything. Hooking an arm around her waist, I pull her into me and claim her lips in a kiss that I hope tells her everything.

Her arms wrap around my shoulders and her fingers bury into my hair.

The hoots and hollers behind me have me laughing against her mouth.

"SCCCCOOOORRRREEEEE," they all shout together and Emma hides her face in my chest.

"Don't worry, I'll make sure they all have extra conditioning at the next practice."

She looks up at me. "I have no idea what that means, but don't be too hard on them, I'm kind of glad they found me."

Let the Season Begin!!

A little sneak peek

SLIDE TACKLED

Book 1 - Storm Series

Kasen

Today's win on the soccer field is the creator of tonight's pool party. Ryker, one of our defense players, invites everyone over after each home game win. The setup he has here is insane. Large pool, sporting a huge rock formation waterfall and bar extended into it, along with an additional bar and entertainment area complete with large screen television and fire pit. Let's not forget the half-size soccer field he has out here as well.

The music is loud, I can feel its vibration through the bar chair I'm sitting on.

A hand on my shoulder has my attention going to my right.

Ryker is standing there handing me a bottle of beer. "Man, if it wasn't for you, this party wouldn't be happening. Amazing saves today." He taps the neck of his bottle to mine.

"No thanks to my defense."

"Ouch, man." His hand goes to his chest as if in pain.

Three years ago I made it to the Major League Soccer and signed on with the Colorado Storm as their goalkeeper. The team didn't know what to do with their new deaf goalkeeper, all except Ryker, and we hit it off pretty quick.

There were smiles and nods, but no one approached me the first day in the locker room. I figured the coaches would have let the team know that I could communicate just fine, but I quickly realized they didn't when Ryker approached me and introduced himself in a way I will always appreciate.

He walked up and tapped me on the shoulder, grabbing my attention. Turning, I found him standing there pounding on his chest. I realized it was his sign for, "I'm". Next he held up a paper with his name on it and waved it in front of my face, then held out his hand for me to shake.

I have to say, Ryker, out of everyone, probably is the one who demands the most attention on the team, but he is a great guy and the only one who even attempted to communicate with me.

I think the best part was his expression when I said, "It's nice to meet you, I'm Kasen."

His eyes went wide with shock. "Wait, I thought they said you were deaf. You talk a little funny, but you talk. So I'm guessing not deaf."

"Yes, I'm deaf, but I read lips, and yes, I've been told I talk a little funny."

We've been great friends since then.

"There is a ton of beer and I'm expecting you to have fun, not just sit here all night."

Stretching, I feel where I took a knee to the ribs today as I went one-on-one with the forward from the other team.

"I'm not staying long." I point at my side.

Ryker points at my ribs with his bottle. "I may have to admit, that might have been my fault."

I give him the whole "you think" look. "You mean that slide-tackle you missed?"

"I said sorry, not my fault you can't hear. Next time I'll sign it."

Rolling my eyes, I take a long drink from my beer.

"He didn't score." Ryker laughs, slapping me on the back and then walking away.

Joking aside, Ryker is a great defense player, probably one of the best in the league, so being able to give him a hard time about something he missed is rare and I make sure to rub it in on those few and in between times that he does mess up. However, my inability to hear, he is always making jokes about.

Most of the players have either brought their "otherhalves" or a girl they picked up somewhere. I, on the other hand, wasn't even planning on coming by. My plans for tonight were to take a long shower and relax for the night, but Ryker had other plans for my evening. Telling me that I'm the reason why this evening was even happening and that I better be here.

I'm realizing now that I should have just stayed home. The more I sit here the more my ribs are yelling at me. Getting up from the chair, I make my way through the crowd deciding that I better move around a little, stretch the muscles, maybe sneak out for the evening.

Walking over to the brightly lit-up half field, I pick up one of the soccer balls and toss it up a couple of times. Looking over at the goal, I still have a hard time sometimes with the reality that this is my life. I'm getting the chance to play the sport that I've loved since I can remember and get paid to do it. Not many people can say they love their work.

Tossing the ball up once again, it's taken before I catch it again.

A woman walks in front of me tossing the ball between her two hands

The ball looks comfortable in her hands. She's played before.

"Remembering the game." She smiles at me and I swear something just punched me in the chest.

Shaking my head no, I point down at my side, "I have a reminder of the game and it's probably going to be around for a few days."

"It was a great save, though." The ball juggles off her knee down to her feet a couple of times and back into her hands. "Guess that means I couldn't interest you in a little one-on-one."

"As much as I would like to, I'm going to have to decline the chance. Game in a couple of days."

She takes a couple of steps toward me. "I've been told that you are deaf."

I study her for a moment, she must be here with one of the guys, which means this chocolate-brown-eyed beauty standing in front of me is off limits.

"Was that a question?"

She shakes her head no. "I'm sorry, I didn't mean to make that sound rude, I'm just surprised is all."

"Why, because I can talk? Deaf, not mute."

Her cheeks turn a slight shade of red and her eyes leave mine and look down at the ball, her fingers tracing the pattern on the ball.

"I'm sorry. I didn't mean for that to come across as I'm thinking it might have."

Her eyes come back up to mine. "Why are you out here and not over there with everyone else?" She tosses her head back to the crowd at the pool.

"I needed to stretch a little." I point at the ball, "You play?"

"All the way through college."

"What position?"

She smiles, tossing the ball up and catching it once again. "Keeper. I fully understand the hazards of playing the position." She uses the ball and points in the direction of my stomach.

Movement to my right grabs my attention and I watch as Ryker walks around me and stands next to the woman.

His arm slings around her shoulders and he leans in, kissing her on the temple.

Damn, she's here with Ryker, definitely off limits.

The woman rolls her eyes, but her smile becomes wider. She cradles the ball under one arm and her other one goes around Ryker's waist.

"What are you two doing out here all alone?" Ryker asks, accusing eyes bouncing between myself and the woman.

I adjust my feet a little, taking a couple of small steps back, hoping that my actions prove to Ryker that I'm not trying to move in on his girl.

"I was trying to get him to do a little one-on-one, but he refused."

Not going to lie, I'm a little envious of Ryker right now.

"Going to warn you, she's good."

You can see the pride shining through Ryker's eyes as he looks down at the woman plastered to his side. How have I not heard about her yet?

"Hey, I'm going to head out."

"Man, it's still early."

Ignoring his statement, I say, "It was nice meeting you…"

"Devyn." She fills in the blank.

"Devyn…" I repeat.

Before Ryker can say anything else to try and convince me to stay, I quickly turn and make my way to my truck.

I purposely parked on the street so that I knew I could leave when I wanted to and not be blocked in by all the other's vehicles.

Hopping up into the driver's seat, I wince a little as my ribs remind me that today's game was a brutal one. Leaning forward slowly, I place the key in the ignition and feel the vibration of the engine through my seat as my truck starts up.

Letting it idol for a moment, I sit back in the seat and allow the pounding in my ribs to work its way out for a moment. I knew I should have stayed home tonight. Of course that would have resulted in me not meeting Devyn.

What am I thinking? I shake my head at myself. She's my best friend's girl. I'm still wondering why he hasn't said anything about her, though. They seemed pretty familiar which I would guess that would mean they didn't just meet.

Now that I think about it, it couldn't have been that long ago. We were just here for another after-game party about a week ago and at that party she wasn't the girl he had wrapped around him all night.

Ryker, in the three years that I've known him, could only be defined as a player, on the field and off.

Devyn isn't his usual type either. She wasn't wearing the skimpiest bikini she could find, and she wasn't hanging all over him all night long. Actually, up to the moment he walked over to the field to join us, I never saw her with him once. I'm having a hard time believing someone has tamed my friend that fast, but after meeting her, I have to give it to my friend. He's smarter than I thought, she is definitely one you make the changes for.

ABOUT THE AUTHOR

USA Today Bestselling Author, Tonya Clark, lives in Southern California with her hot firefighter hubby and two amazing daughters. She writes contemporary romance featuring second chance, sports, MC, shifters, suspense, and deaf culture-inspired by her youngest daughter.

When not hiding in the office writing, Tonya has the amazing job of photographing hot cover models, coaching multiple soccer teams, and running her day job.

Tonya believes everyone deserves their Happily Ever After!

Sign-up for Tonya's newsletter at www.tonyaclarkbooks.com for book news and you can find all of her books on Amazon.

- instagram.com/authortonyaclark
- amazon.com/author/tonyaclark
- bookbub.com/authors/tonya-clark
- goodreads.com/authortonyaclark
- tiktok.com/@authortonyaclark

ALSO BY TONYA CLARK

Sign of Love Series

Silent Burn

Silent Distraction

Silent Protection

Silent Forgiveness

Sign of Love Circle

Shift

For the Love of Brayden

Storm Series

Slide Tackled

Off Side Trap (Releasing 2024)

Standalone

Retake

Entangled Rivals

Driven Roads

Healing Tristan

Hidden Flight

Shame on Me

Honeymoon After All (Releasing End of 2023)

Made in the USA
Columbia, SC
10 February 2024